The Nicholas Stories

Luigi and the Lost Wish

Written by Harry B. Knights

Original Artwork by Calico World Entertainment

Publisher - Larry D. Faw

Zweig Knights Publishing

A Subsidiary of Studio City Holding Corp.

Limited 1st Edition

Registered Number: 5974

10,000 limited first editions published: November 1, 2000

The Nicholas Stories

The Nicholas Stories

Luigi and the Lost Wish

Written by Harry B. Knights

Original Artwork by Calico World Entertainment

Publisher - Larry D. Faw

Zweig Knights Publishing

A Subsidiary of Studio City Holding Corp.

3

Dedication

To Lou Rotunno, our very own Luigi. A special Elf and good friend.

Printed and bound in Mexico

This publication is designed to provide inspiration to young and old, and, is designed in its content for all peoples of the world. It is being published with the understanding that the publisher is not engaged in political intent, and, is being sold to encourage peace and love for humanity.

ISBN: 1-58114-250-1

Cataloging-in Publication Data

Knights, Harry B.

    The Nicholas Stories: Luigi and the Lost Wish
        P.cm

Summary: A wish is lost and Luigi blames his friend. Once the wish is found, it is Luigi who discovers a most unselfish way to fulfill it.

[1. Christmas--Fiction. 2. Santa Claus--Fiction. 3. The North Pole--Fiction. 4. Religion--Inspirational. 5. Family Values--Fiction. 6. Saint Nicholas. 7. Kris Kringle.]
1. Title

The text was set in Goudy Old style.
The display type was set in Old English Text and Goudy Old style.
The interior pages were printed on 80# Patina Matte.
The jacket wrap was printed on 100# stock with gloss laminate.
Production photography by Hans Kaczmarek, German Master Photographer and Son.
Color separations by Blackhawk Color Corporation.
Printed and bound by R.R. Donnelley & Sons Company.

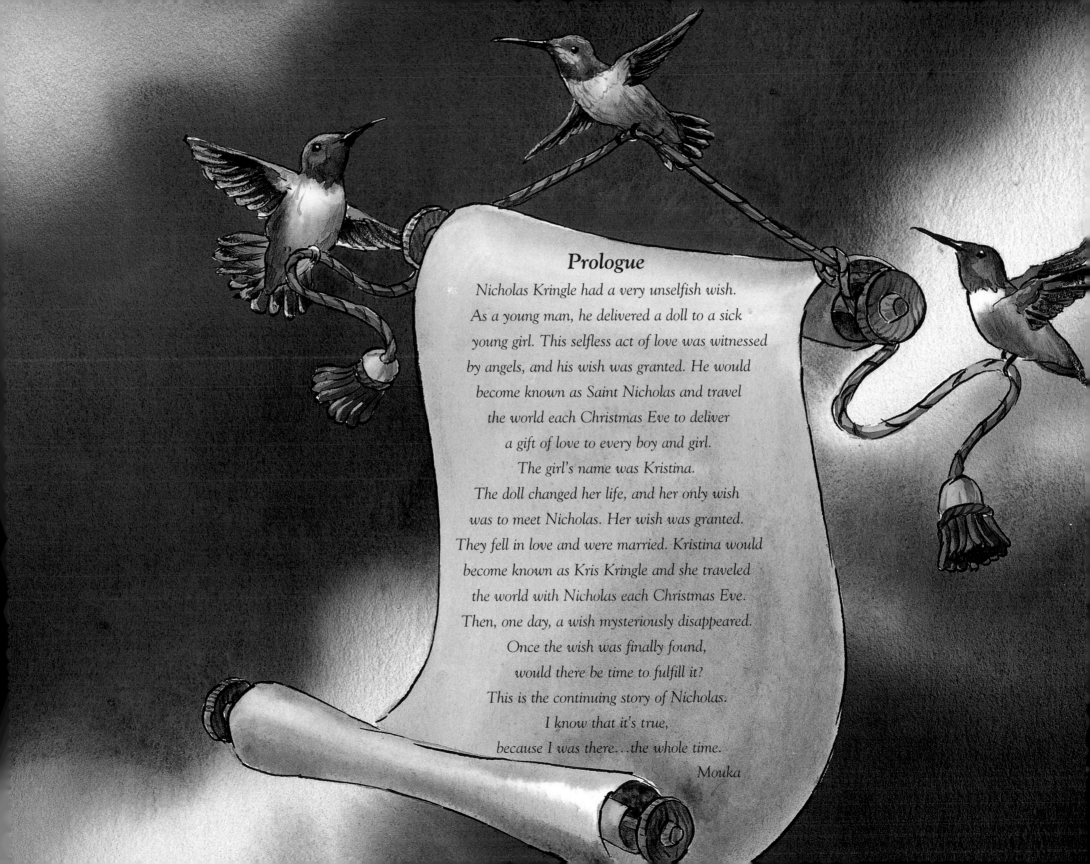

Prologue

Nicholas Kringle had a very unselfish wish.
As a young man, he delivered a doll to a sick
young girl. This selfless act of love was witnessed
by angels, and his wish was granted. He would
become known as Saint Nicholas and travel
the world each Christmas Eve to deliver
a gift of love to every boy and girl.
The girl's name was Kristina.
The doll changed her life, and her only wish
was to meet Nicholas. Her wish was granted.
They fell in love and were married. Kristina would
become known as Kris Kringle and she traveled
the world with Nicholas each Christmas Eve.
Then, one day, a wish mysteriously disappeared.
Once the wish was finally found,
would there be time to fulfill it?
This is the continuing story of Nicholas.
I know that it's true,
because I was there...the whole time.

Mouka

Nicholas Kringle became known as Saint Nicholas. He married Kristina and, of course, most of us know her as Kris Kringle. They lived happily together in The Land Beyond Yon with all the Elves. There was Goe, Luigi, Mayor Ono, ….and of course me, Mouka.

You may already know that I have been Nicholas' best friend since he was a child and I am the official storyteller of the Nicholas Stories. This is something that I really enjoy doing.

As you may recall, Goe finally captured the Spirit of Christmas. Since that night several years ago, Goe learned all he could about Christmas. There was only one answer he did not know…"What was the very first Christmas gift?" He asked, but no one could give him the answer. This bothered Goe. He knew there was an answer out there somewhere…..

Did you notice Luigi's hat? Luigi wore that big hat for a reason. He had big hair, really big hair. His hair was so big that he needed a special hat.

Everyone knew that he was very proud of his big hair. In fact, he would mention it every chance he had. Luigi could not even walk by a mirror without stopping to admire it.

One day, while Luigi was sorting wishes, Goe entered the room with a box of silver bells. "Nicholas wanted these kept in the wishroom until Christmas Eve. Where shall I put them?" he asked. Luigi was busy admiring his hair as he pointed to a place beside his desk. "I think my hair looks extra nice today, do you think so too?" asked Luigi.

A bird flew in to deliver another child's wish. The letter that Luigi had just opened blew onto the floor.

Goe could not see the letter and he put the box down on top of it.

"Yes Luigi, your hair looks nice, but may I ask you a question? What was the first Christmas gift?" "I have no idea," said Luigi as he admired his hair. Goe shrugged his shoulders and left the room.

15

Luigi went back to sorting wishes and realized that the letter was missing. He looked around the room and did not see the letter.

He decided right away that Goe must have taken it!

Luigi went straight to Goe and demanded that he return the letter. Goe had no idea what Luigi was talking about, but it did not matter. Luigi was certain that Goe had taken the letter and he refused to believe Goe. The other Elves figured that Luigi was right. After all, Goe had done this sort of thing before.

Goe begged them to believe him, but they would not listen. This made Goe very sad. He had not done anything wrong, but no one would even speak to him.

Luigi told Nicholas what had happened. Goe told Nicholas
that he did not take the letter and Nicholas believed him.

Nicholas told Luigi that he should go back to the wishroom and find the missing letter, because Goe was innocent. Luigi never did search for the letter. After all, he was still certain that Goe had taken it.

The Elves all stopped speaking to Goe. They were certain he was guilty. Even though Nicholas believed in Goe, the Elves did not. This made Goe feel sad and lonely.

That night, while Goe was outside, a beautiful Light shone down. It was the Christmas Star! The Star appeared to be on the very top of a tree and its' Light made the snow on the branches glitter and sparkle. Goe was reminded that no one is truly alone. We are loved, each and every one of us.

Goe finally knew what the first Christmas gift was. He wanted to share the news
with the other Elves, but they were not speaking to him. Goe had an idea.

Each day, he would work on his special project. No one asked what he was doing, after all, no one was speaking to him. Day after day, he worked and worked. The Elves still did not believe in Goe, but it no longer mattered. Goe knew that he was loved and he wanted to share that love.

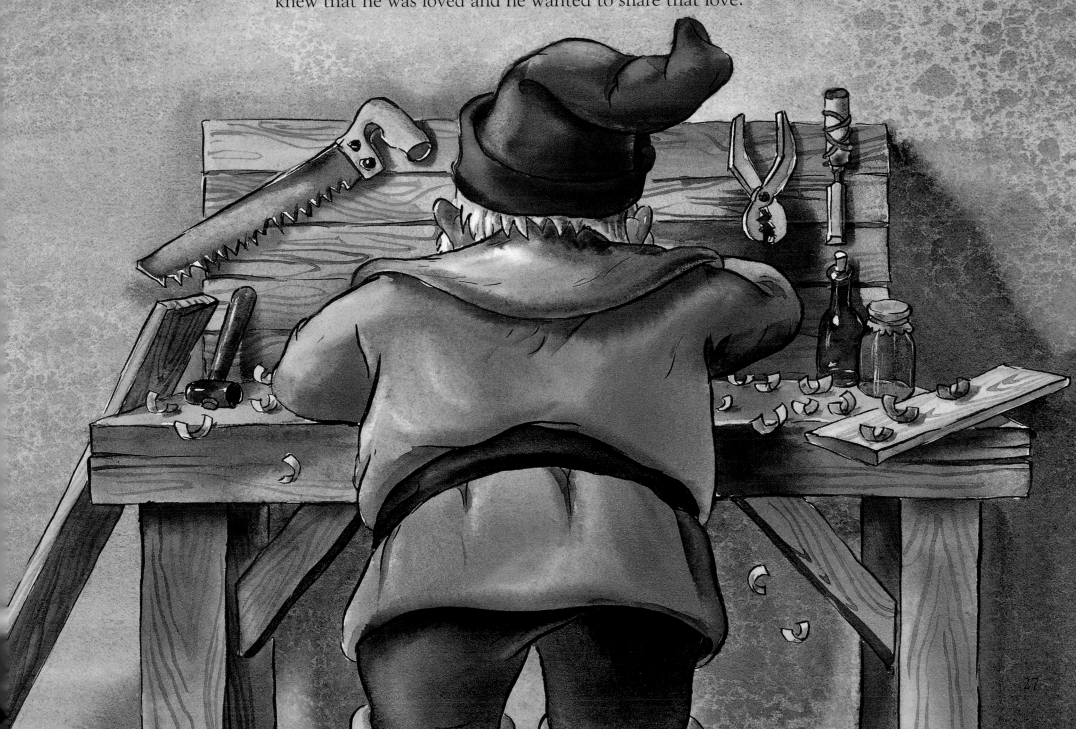

The weeks passed, and finally it was the day before Christmas. The Elves loaded the sleigh as Nicholas and Kris went to the wishroom to get the box of silver bells. When Nicholas picked up the box, Kris noticed the lost wish on the floor. They read the wish:

Dear Santa,
(As Saint Nicholas was commonly called),

My sister has been
so sick that her hair
has fallen out.

She does not believe
that you can help her,
but I know that you can.
My only wish for Christmas
is for her to be happy.

Please help her.

Thank You.

Nicholas and Kris were very upset.

Nicholas called the Elves into the wishroom and told them what had happened. The Elves knew they had been wrong about Goe and they all apologized. **Luigi felt worse than anyone.** Had he only searched for the wish rather than blame his friend, there would have been time for Nicholas to find a solution for "the lost wish."

Goe gave him a big hug and told him not to worry.

Luigi had an idea. He whispered something to Kris and then left the room.

Lost wish or not, it was Christmas Eve and time for Saint Nicholas and Kris Kringle to start their deliveries. Luigi handed Kris a package and she climbed onto the sleigh with Nicholas. "Up, up and away!" they shouted as they headed into the evening sky. The Elves all cheered and waved as the couple waved back.

Later that night, they arrived at the home of the little girl who had lost her hair. Kris opened Luigi's package. Luigi had cut off his beautiful hair to make a wig for the little girl.

Kris placed the wig on the girl's head as she slept. Nicholas and Kris then left to finish their deliveries.

Finally, Nicholas and Kris arrived back home and all the Elves cheered.

Goe had a surprise! He led everyone to a special place. He was about to share his news. There, under the tree with the Christmas Star shining down, was the project he had been working on. It was a manger scene carved of wood. The very first Christmas gift was the birth of Christ; a demonstration of the greatest love anyone could possibly imagine.

It was such a beautiful sight that everyone took their hats off, in reverence. Everyone noticed that Luigi's hair was almost all gone.

Nicholas told them what Luigi had done. They knew what a special sacrifice Luigi had made, and they all clapped for him.

That night, the Elves slept soundly, even as Nicholas and Kris had work to do.
They wanted to give each of the Elves a gift. Kris had an idea

They put a gift in each sock and hung them on the
mantle of the fireplace in the wishroom.

When the Elves woke up the next morning, they were very upset to discover that their socks were missing. "Who would take our socks?" they asked each other.

They certainly were not about to accuse anyone; they had learned *that* lesson the day before. They decided to ask Nicholas to solve the mystery.

He invited them into the wishroom. They immediately spotted their socks hanging on the mantle. They each ran to their own sock to find a gift inside. They were very excited and they were very happy. After all, they were accustomed to giving gifts, not receiving them.

Inside Luigi's sock was a new hat.

Luigi was still somewhat embarrassed by his general lack of hair. He put his new hat on and Kris kissed him right on top of his head! She told him that he was more handsome than he had ever been.

Luigi knew that he had been silly to be so proud of his hair. After all, what you look like makes little difference. It is what you have in your heart, that really matters.

Acknowledgements

With special thanks to the many special friends and artists who have contributed to the publication of this Limited First Edition of "The Nicholas Stories: Luigi and the Lost Wish ".

A special thanks to Harry Knights for the labor of his love, and to Christine Knights, an excellent Elf and special friend, to Betty and Harry Knights Jr., for their loyal and enthusiastic support. To Charlie Flood for staying the course; to Doris Hefler, Phil Testa, Steve Gonzalez, Vincent and Mahruh Neville, Henry Scheuring, Jim and Doris Courchaine and Andrew C. Rigrod, all who in their special way, saw the vision as it turned into reality.

To Tom and Claudia Burton, Joel Fajnor, Chavdar Chushev, and, all the Calico Creations' crew, whose beautiful paintings tell a story within our story.

To Hans Kaczmarek, Master German Photographer and Son, whose knowledge of film, the love of art and the persistence to capture the color palette and illumination of our paintings.

To the entire staff of Blackhawk Color Corporation, whose trained eyes and technical expertise brought to life the brilliance of our paintings.

To Lou and JoAnn Rotunno, Patrick and Nancy Keenan, George and Edwina Worsley, Yoshiro and Sueko Oishi, Alison and Beth Donovan, Norman Godheim, Randy DeFazio, Thomas Rotunno, Alan and Jacklyn Schmetzer, Stephanie and Richard Gehring, Rebecca Womble, Elizabeth Rotunno, Mark Mazzone, Linda Hyer, Jill Ressler, Mark Kasrel, Kevin and Karen Hand, Robert and Josephine Tomasulo, Sheila Wessner, Amy McCallum, Rene Gandelman, Michael Long, Brad McKinney, Ralph and Patricia Rotunno, Harriet Segal, Thomas Steele, Mike Brown, Jan Kenny and family, Kathy Gomberg, Al Golden, James Petroff, James Edmonson, Warren Schmidt, Richard and Ellen Stupak, David West, James and Bonnie Parsons, Ross Hagstoc, Henry and Christine Coleman, James McDade, Anthony Latona, Edna Shields, Harold Markle, Steven Passion, Brad Yoder, Leonard Platnick, Marcus Barth, Vito and Jean Magarelli, Robert and Jennifer Carmignani, Dante S. Alberi, Darlene Calzon-Barror, Christopher Ferguson, James Rowe, Lawrence Kirsch, Gerald Weinberg, Alex Frackoff, Hope Victor, Christopher Carpino, Bruce Moneta, Denise Conti, Arnold Weiss, Craig Martin, Naomi Marcus Zebrick, Tim and Lisa Zuffi, B.J. Fitzgerald, Loretta Conti, Melissa Kopolow, Thomas O'Brien, Vito and Jean Magarelli, Wendy and Andy Johanson, Alena Whitt, Ed Beckett, Michelle Rotunno, Virginia Hobkirk, Linda Kay Hobkirk, Charlotte Morello, Cynthia Patterson, Shirley Fargas, Raymond Smith, Karen Friedman Kravitt, Gregory Zambrycki, George Cantor, Daniel Bowerman, Elaine Axlerod, Peter Moneta, Leonard Danzig, Irvin Smiler, Joan Frey-Boytim, Phyllis Poe Kenny, Suzana & Kendal Schmidt, Margaret and Robert Schmidt, Larry, Laura and Susan Green, Peter Moneta, Robert Bell, Michael Quinlan, Leroy Moyer, Scott Borden, Dolly Friedman, Paul and Lorraine Langenbuch, Mary Ann Horst, Steven Hobkirk, Toby Schmidt, Susan Borden, Edward A. Rosboschil, Anne Oleynick David Kravit, Renate Rotunno, Frank Leto, James O'Brien, Diana Raph, Judith Kuhns, Harry Kaplan, Louis Kopolow, George Graham, Philip Litwak, Stanley Schneider, Audrey Meredith, Steve Napiecek, James O'Brien, James A. Farmer, Harry Quinlan, Michael Tyson, Robert Smith, Wilba Gae and Tom Smith, Brian McGuire, Kenneth C. Welsh, Jr., Pamela Rosenberg, Harvey Spector, Beth Schlein, Donna Moyer, Michael Friedman, Audrey Drenios, David Rotunno, John Churchill, and, David J. Levenson.

The Nicholas Stories:
"The Boy With A Wish"
"The First Flight of Saint Nicholas"
"The Maiden Voyage of Kris Kringle"

"Luigi and the Lost Wish"
"A Christmas Without Snow"
"The Child that Christmas Forgot"

Zweig Knights Publishing Corporation
Copyright 2000, 1999, 1998, 1997, 1996, 1970 ™
the end..